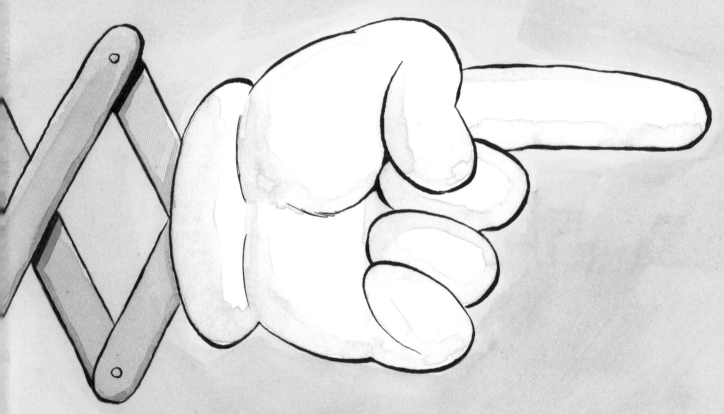

RUBE GOLDBERG's
SIMPLE NORMAL HUMDRUM SCHOOL DAY

BY **JENNIFER GEORGE**

ILLUSTRATED BY
ED STECKLEY

INVENTION DESIGN BY
**JOSEPH HERSCHER
& ED STECKLEY**

ABRAMS BOOKS FOR YOUNG READERS
NEW YORK

ACKNOWLEDGMENTS

First and foremost, I want to thank Charles Kochman—my brilliant editor at Abrams, who had a vision for this book long before I did. Charlie, you are my kindred spirit and the reason for all of this. Thank you for always having faith in Rube. To Ed Steckley, my friend and the brave artist who took on the tall task of assuming Rube's hand—you are masterful and nimble, and your spirit for the work brings out the best in everyone, and most especially what's on the page. Then there's Joseph Herscher, also a dear friend, who thinks like my grandfather and whose humor, elegance, and grace are evident in every machine he designs and every machine he builds. Joseph, I may be the keeper of the flame, but you *are* the flame. Others I must thank who helped get this book from our minds and into your hands are: Laura Nolan, Bob Bookman, Susan Van Metre, Andrew Smith, Chad Beckerman, Tree Abraham, Samantha Hoback, Alison Gervais, Jill Smith, Jon Reichman, Dr. Shawn Jordan, Drew Wischer, Kathleen Felix, Janine Napierkowski, Marilyn Bellock, and Brand Central's Mark Otero. Lastly, to my "Papa Rube"—it takes a small army of creatives to re-create and imitate what you did alone. How on earth did you do it?

The illustrations in this book were made with pen and ink and watercolor on Strathmore.

Cataloging-in-Publication Data has been applied for and may be obtained from the Library of Congress.

ISBN 978-1-4197-2558-6

Book design by Tree Abraham and Chad W. Beckerman

Printed and bound in China
10 9 8 7 6 5 4 3 2 1

Abrams Books for Young Readers are available at special discounts when purchased in quantity for premiums and promotions as well as fundraising or educational use. Special editions can also be created to specification. For details, contact specialsales@abramsbooks.com or the address below.

ABRAMS The Art of Books
115 West 18th Street, New York, NY 10011
abramsbooks.com

TO THE DREAMERS AND BUILDERS,
PAST, PRESENT, AND FUTURE,
WHO SCAFFOLD MY HEART—
YOU KNOW WHO YOU ARE

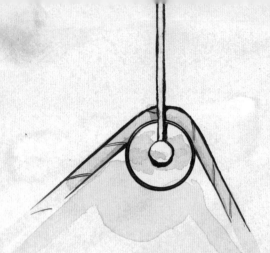
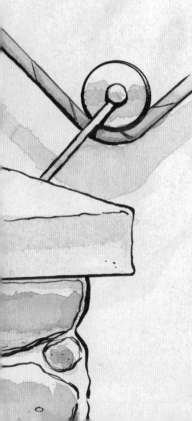

It's early on an ordinary morning, down an ordinary street, in an ordinary house. And for a just a few more minutes in the Goldberg home, all is quiet. Rube is asleep.

But as soon as the sun rises and shines through his bedroom window, you'll see that Rube is no ordinary boy. He is an inventor and a tinkerer, and he builds epic contraptions. For Rube, up is down, in is out, and no is yes. Maybe he likes doing things the hard way because it's more fun. Or maybe he just sees the world a little differently than most of us. But you can decide for yourself. Here's how Rube Goldberg begins this particular simple, normal, humdrum school day.

RUBE GOLDBERG'S SIMPLE WAY TO WAKE UP IN THE MORNING

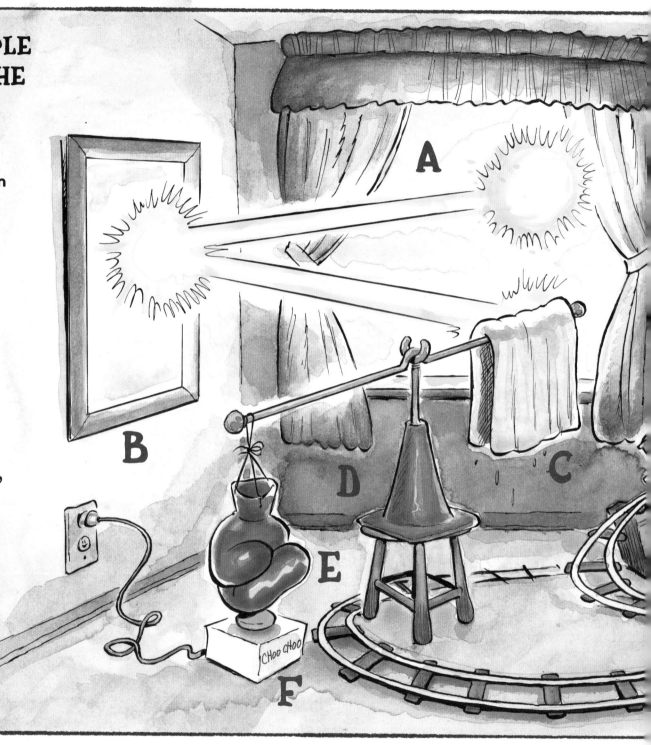

SUNLIGHT (A) shines through bedroom window and bounces off **MIRROR (B)**, drying yesterday's **BATH TOWEL (C)**. Towel dries and gets lighter, causing **SCALE (D)** to tip down, lowering **BOXING GLOVE (E)**, which turns on **POWER SWITCH (F)**, starting **MODEL TRAIN (G)**. Train chugs up hill and launches off pile of books, landing on the power button of **VACUUM CLEANER (H)**. Vacuum sucks up crumpled **PAPER (I)**, tightening string, causing **PITCHER (J)** to tip and spill cold water on top of Rube—waking him up from a sound sleep.

AN EASY WAY TO GET DRESSED

Rube slides down RAILING (A) into pants and sneakers, landing on BELLOWS (B), which blasts puff of air onto SLEEPING CAT (C). Startled cat leaps off scale, lowering IRON (D) onto AIR PUMP (E). Planet Earth BEACH BALL (F) inflates, causing pile of DIRTY CLOTHES (G) to slide into LAUNDRY BASKET (H), which weighs down strings and pulls open PLIERS (I), allowing shirt to drop onto Rube. Rushing into the kitchen for breakfast, Rube passes through DOORWAY (J), quickly brushing his hair.

AN EXCELLENT WAY TO MAKE BREAKFAST

Rube jumps onto cutting board SEESAW (A). LEMON (B) catapults and turns on HANDHELD VACUUM (C), which sucks in dish towel and knocks over BAG OF FLOUR (D), which falls onto BICYCLE HORN (E). Loud honk wakes HEN (F), who suddenly lays several EGGS (G). Eggs roll down ramp and turn on veggie-filled BLENDER (H) before ending up in frying pan. Smoothie splatters CURTAINS (I), which get heavier and pull down curtain rod, lowering HELPING HAND (J) and pushing down bread into TOASTER (K). When ready, toast pops up and slides down butter-smeared SLING CHAIR (L), which launches two slices of perfectly buttered toast in the air for Rube to catch as he runs out the door.

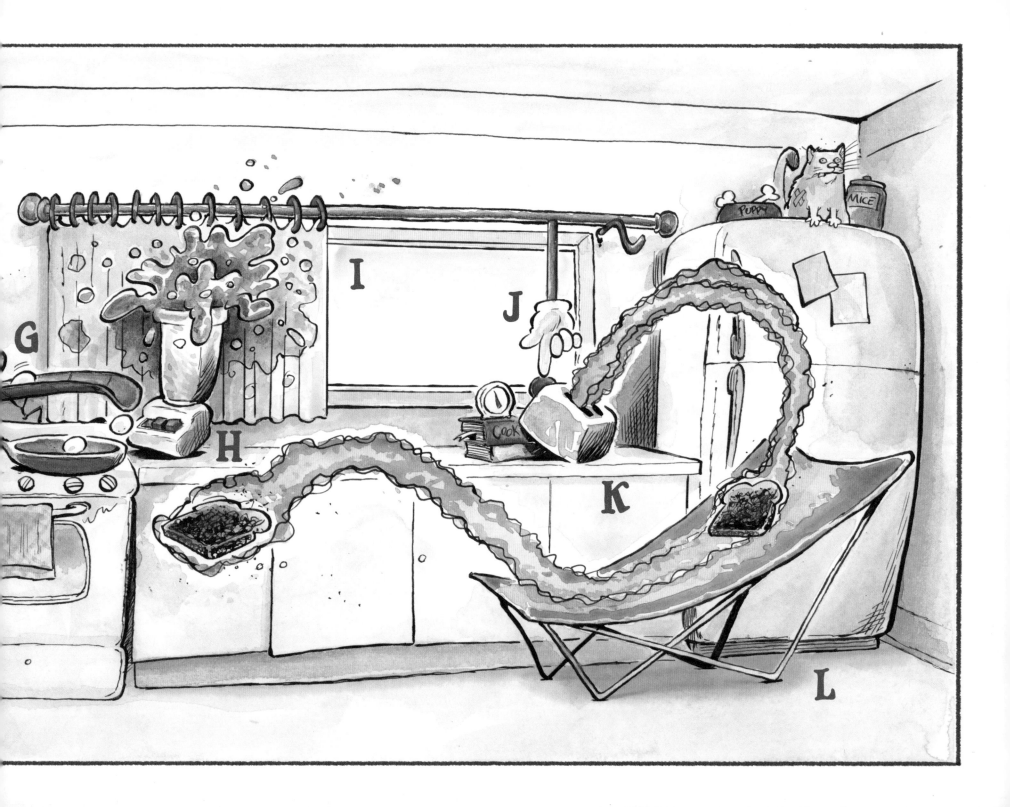

A SUREFIRE WAY TO CATCH THE SCHOOL BUS

Jumping on **EXERCISE TRAMPOLINE** (**A**), Rube leaps out the front door, grabbing **ZIP LINE** (**B**). His foot bumps **CHAIR** (**C**), knocking over **PITCHER OF ORANGE JUICE** (**D**) onto **BARBEQUE GRILL** (**E**), which smokes out hungry **RACCOON** (**F**), who thinks it's time for hot dogs. The raccoon steps out of tree and onto **BRANCH CLIPPERS** (**G**), which cut string, releasing **BOOT** (**H**) that kicks **YOGA BALL** (**I**) into open **BUS DOORS** (**J**), jamming them. This keeps the bus from moving while impatient driver grumbles, and Rube flings himself off zip line and onto the bus.

AN AWESOME WAY TO OPEN A SCHOOL LOCKER

Late for class, Rube runs down hallway and grabs **STRING (A)**, which yanks **HAMMER (B)** into **PIGGY BANK (C)**. Smashed pig releases **COINS (D)**, which roll down chute and into **GUMBALL MACHINE (E)**. A stream of **GUMBALLS (F)** pours into **BUCKET (G)**. As it gets heavier, bucket pulls down **SPRING MECHANISM (H)**, lifting **HELPING HAND (I)** which pulls up **LATCH (J)** and opens both the locker door and the cracker-covered **DICTIONARY (K)** at the same time. Falling **CRACKERS (L)** excite the always-hungry **CAFETERIA BIRD (M)**, who swings forward to catch the snack, lifting her **MAGNETIC SNEAKERS (N)** until they attach to metal door, swinging open the locker.

A GOOF-PROOF WAY TO SNEAK INTO CLASS LATE

Rube opens **BIOLOGY LAB DOOR** (**A**), allowing hungry **GOAT** (**B**) to enter. As goat happily eats organic **CASHEWS** (**C**), he bobs his head up and down until his horns pierce a hole in **SANDBAG** (**D**). Bag gets lighter, and **LEVER** (**E**) lowers **BROOM** (**F**), releasing tippy shelf so that **CROQUET BALL** (**G**) falls off. This causes **METAL BALLS** (**H**) to clack back and forth, knocking **SCIENCE TROPHY** (**I**) off shelf and onto **TRIGGER** (**J**) for **CROSSBOW** (**K**). This shoots **ARROW** (**L**) into **INFLATED TIRE** (**M**), so that slowly escaping air propels Rube into biology class on his skateboard.

AN EPIC WAY TO MAKE A PAINTING

Rube releases **ROPE (A)**, dropping **BUCKET OF SAND (B)** onto **TRASH PEDAL (C)**. Lid springs open, hurling **RUBBER DUCK (D)** into **MALLET (E)**, which slams down on **PAINT TUBE (F)**. Large dollop of paint hits **CERAMIC MUG (G)**, causing it to fall and hit **"ON" SWITCH (H)** of **FAN (I)**. Spinning **TUBE (J)** connected to **BELT (K)** turns mechanical **LAWN MOWER BLADES (L)**, allowing three **BROOMS (M)** to drag through **PAINT TRAYS (N)** and onto the **CANVAS (O)**, creating an epic painting.

A HANDY WAY TO DUNK A BASKETBALL

Rube positions his **BASKETBALL DUNKER** (A) in place and starts by tipping back his **HELMET** (B), which causes **PAIL OF GOLF BALLS** (C) to spill into a twisty **FUNNEL** (D) and land in upside-down **FOOTBALL HELMET** (E). Golf balls weigh down helmet's spring bottom, tugging **STRING** (F), which pulls **PIN** (G), releasing spring-loaded **HELPING HAND** (H), which dunks **BASKETBALL** (I) easily into **HOOP** (J).

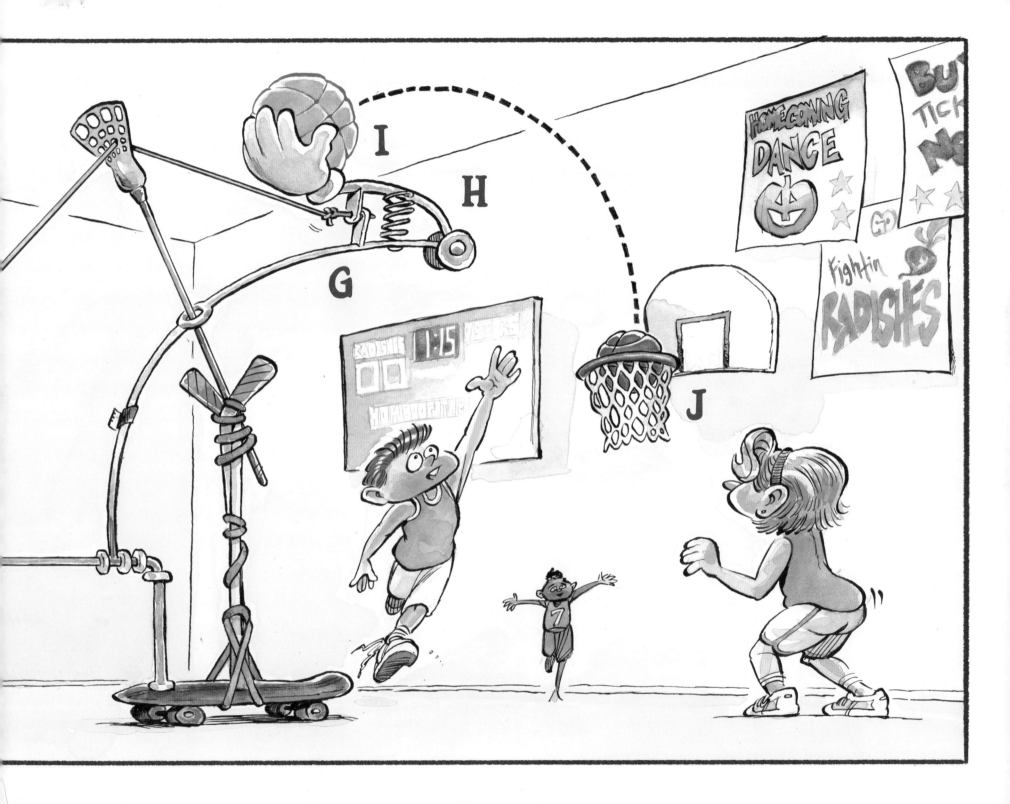

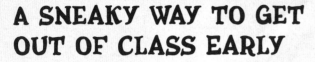

A SNEAKY WAY TO GET OUT OF CLASS EARLY

Rube tugs **WORLD MAP (A)** on table, toppling alphabet **BLOCK TOWER (B)**, which releases **PLANET PENDULUM (C)**, knocking **BOOK (D)** off shelf. Weight of book pulls on string that's tied to **POWER SWITCH (E)**, turning on **FAN (F)**, which blows **PIRATE SHIP WIND EXPERIMENT (G)** into lemonade **WATER COOLER SPIGOT (H)**. This releases a stream of liquid into **CLARINET (I)** and out its finger holes. Worried classroom **RABBIT (J)** thinks it's raining and jumps for cover under umbrella tied to a **BROOM (K)**. Broom tips, and umbrella prong moves the **CLOCK HAND (L)** forward fifteen minutes.

AN EFFORTLESS WAY TO PLAY WITH THE DOG WHILE PRACTICING PIANO

Rube plays piano, pressing **FOOT PEDALS (A)**, which pull **STRINGS (B)**, causing **FEATHER DUSTER (C)** to drag back and forth, sweeping **FLOUR (D)** out of bowl. As bowl gets lighter, the **SCALE (E)** rises, pulling string and causing **PAINTING (F)** to tilt down. Angled picture allows **RUBBER BALL (G)** to roll down edge of frame, onto **CHUTE (H)** and into **PITCHER (I)**. Pitcher drops, pulling string, which lifts **HAT (J)**, revealing **CHEESE (K)** to **BERTHA (L)**, Rube's Siberian Cheesehound. Bertha's **LEASH (M)** pulls revolving **HAT STAND (N)** as she chases her favorite snack, running in circles—creating a never-ending play session for both piano player and pet!

A SPEEDY WAY TO GET ALL OF YOUR HOMEWORK DONE AT THE SAME TIME

As Rube turns page of book, **STRING (A)** pulls down **TREE BRANCH (B)**, causing ripe **APPLE (C)** to fall from tree and into **SOUP LADLE (D)**. This makes **CLOTHES HANGER (E)** tilt down, pulling **STRING (F)**, which uncorks **VINEGAR BOTTLE (G)**. Vinegar pours into baking powder–filled **VOLCANO (H)**, completing Rube's science homework. Erupting volcano ejects molten fluid into **BUCKET (I)**, which lowers and turns **CRANK (J)**, spinning electric potter's wheel, where **HELPING HANDS (K)** shape rotating **CLAY (L)** until Rube's homework for art class is finished.

A NO-BRAINER WAY TO AVOID BABY BROTHER'S FLYING FOOD AT DINNER

Rube's baby brother, Walter, sits in a high chair, playing with his food. When Walter leans forward, his UNDERSHIRT (A) pulls rope, which unties slip-knotted CURTAIN SASH (B), allowing curtain to open and drag across plate of PEANUTS (C). Peanuts fall into BASKET (D), weighing it down, causing WATERING CAN (E) to tip, soaking HANGING PLANT (F). Watered plant gets heavier and pulls down on rope attached to WALL SWITCH (G), turning on CEILING FAN (H). Rotating blades are connected to string tied to a BANANA (I), which hits spring-loaded MECHANISM (J), opening UMBRELLA (K) and shielding Rube from his baby brother's flying food!

A PERFECT WAY TO PUT TOOTHPASTE ON A TOOTHBRUSH

Rube lifts FAUCET HANDLE (A), loosening string, which tips MEASURING CUP (B). Water spills out of cup onto dry BAR OF SOAP (C), making it slippery enough to slide down angled shelf and into FUNNEL (D), then into BUCKET (E). Weight of soap makes the bucket drop, pulling down on towel, which rotates ROD (F) and moves GEARS (G) to turn on SHOWER (H), filling bathtub. As water rises, BEACH BALL (I) floats upward, pushing SQUEEGEE (J), lifting shelf. This causes BOOKS (K) to fall over, knocking BOWLING BALL (L) off shelf and onto TOOTHPASTE TUBE (M), which squirts out a perfect dollop of paste onto Rube's toothbrush.

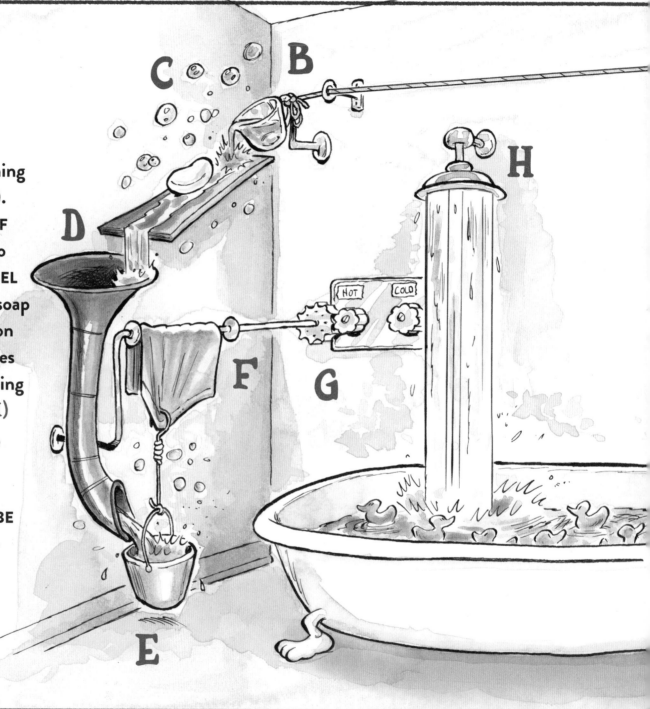

nary day, down an ordinary
rdinary house, it's late at
Goldberg home, all is quiet.

. now it's time to dream.

A SIMPLE WAY TO GO TO BED

Rube finishes reading his favorite book. As he closes it, **STRING** (A) pulls open **DRESSER DRAWER** (B) and out pops a **JACK-IN-THE-BOX** (C), which bumps into shelf of origami **PAPER BALLOONS** (D). This causes **PADLOCK** (E) to fall off shelf and **STRING** (F) to wind around **TELESCOPE EYEPIECE** (G), which rotates and extends, pushing **SOFTBALL** (H) down track. Softball hits **ENCYCLOPEDIA** (I) and rolls into **BIKE HELMET** (J). Weight of softball pulls down on mechanical **CHAIR LEVER** (K), which raises seat. String tied to back of **CHAIR** (L) pulls up **WALL SWITCH** (M), turning off dresser **LIGHT** (N). The string is also connected to **BED** (O), where it pulls **LEVERED ARM** (P) attached to blankets, tucking Rube in for the night.

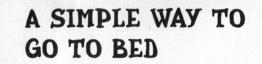

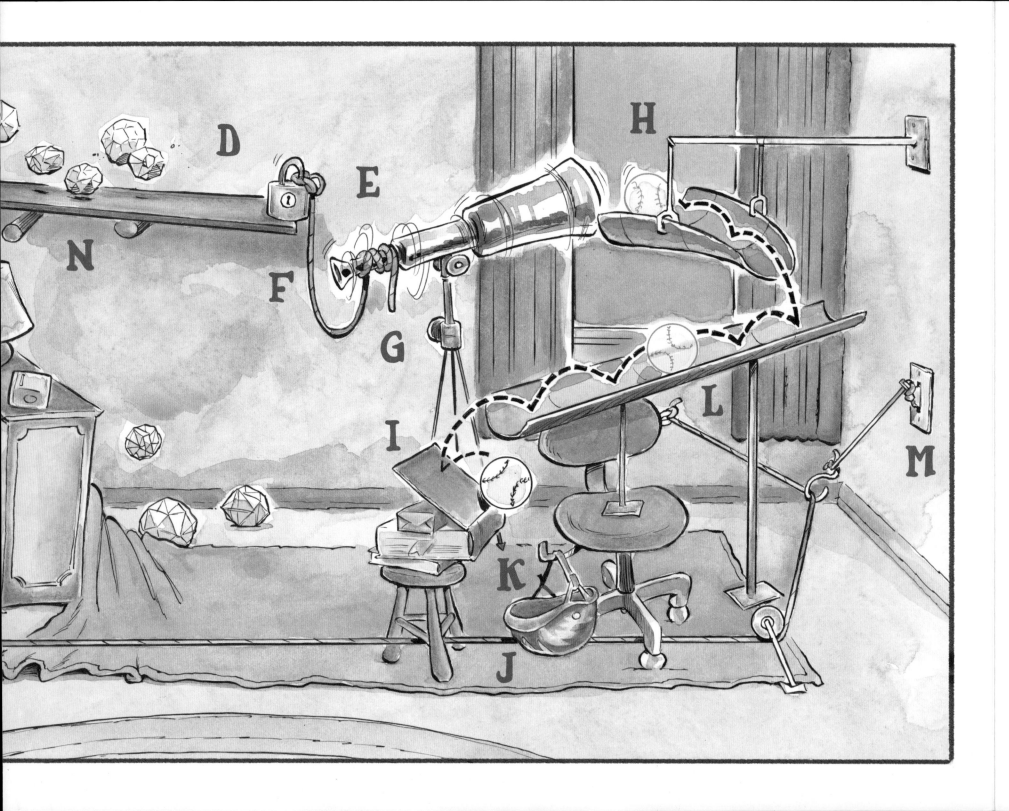

STEM (Science, Technology, Engineering, and Math) and STEAM (the "A" is added for Art) are educational principles that can easily be taught using Rube Goldberg's inventions.

A complex Rube Goldberg Machine is always made up of a series of smaller, simpler machines. These can be created out of everyday items, including levers, pulleys, inclined planes, wedges, springs, pendulums, wheels, and axels.

You can teach the basics of STEM and STEAM by using the illustrations in this book.

If you like to build, tinker, and invent stuff, join a Rube Goldberg Machine Contest! There are competitions for students of all ages.

For more information visit rubegoldberg.com.

Rube Goldberg's Simple Way to Wake Up in the Morning
Pendulum (D), Wheel (G)

An Easy Way to Get Dressed
Pendulum (D), Pulley (H)

An Excellent Way to Make Breakfast
Inclined plane (A), Spring (K)

A Surefire Way to Catch the School Bus
Pulley (B), Wedge (G)

An Awesome Way to Open a School Locker
Pulley (A), Spring (H), Lever (J), Inclined plane (K)

A Goof-Proof Way to Sn
Pulley (D), Pendulum

An Epic Way to Make a F
Pulley (A) and (B), L

A Handy Way to Dunk a
Spring (H)

A Sneaky Way to Get Ou
Pendulum (C), Lever

An Effortless Way to Pla
Lever (A), Pulley (B)

A Speedy Way to Get All
Pendulum (E), Whee

A No-Brainer Way to Av
Pulley (B), Lever (G)

A Perfect Way to Put To
Lever (A), Inclined p

A Simple Way to Go to E
Pulley (A), Spring (C

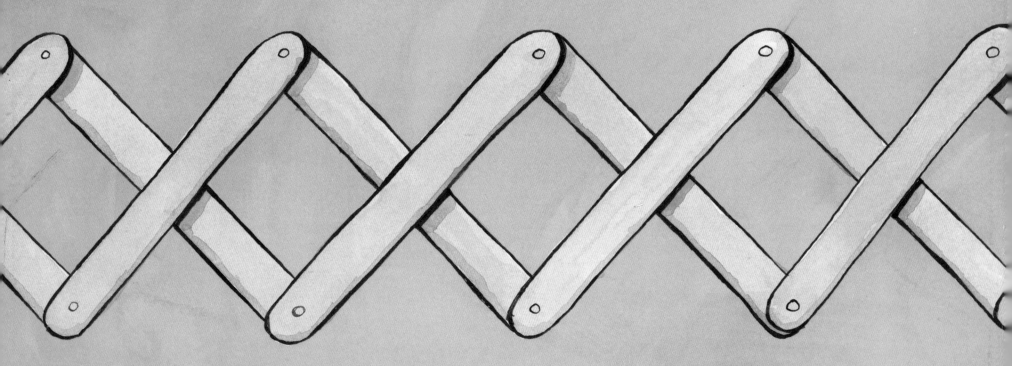